The Who That I Am

by Cynthia Carla
Art by Stephen Aitken

ISBN 978-1-7777391-0-2 (hardcover)
ISBN 978-1-7777391-1-9 (softcover)
ISBN 978-1-7777391-2-6 (ebook)

Book Design and Ebook by Jill Ronsley, suneditwrite.com

Published by C&C Enterprises
Vancouver, Canada

Printed and bound in Canada

Cynthia Carla

When I found my true self by following my heart I discovered the "who" that I was—the true essence of myself that was hidden away for many years. My inner light began to sparkle and shine through. This light grew and grew, and it helped bring this book, *The Who That I Am*, into existence.

Visit me at cynthiacarla.com or on Facebook (The Who That I Am - Children's Book) and Instagram (@cynthiacarla_ author).

Stephen Aitken

Hi! I was a biological illustrator, drawing bugs, trees, flowers and animals. I now write and illustrate books from my studio that I share with a bashful house gecko and an odd orange-eared mouse.

Four facts about me: I can't remember ever not painting or writing. I co-founded an environmental charity to help conserve our natural world. I love to buy books and art supplies. Ants (and sand) in my food creep me out.

Thank you, thank you, to every soul
Who helped me accomplish every goal.

Lifting me up and helping me through.
Thank you, Universe, for being so true.

To my bunnies and babe, my whole heart,
I love you always—"never tear us apart."

To my Papa, now an angel above,
Thank you for sharing all of your love.

And …

To the amazing YOU reading this page—
Be brave and be ready to take the stage.

Love yourself; let your spirit shine through.
The world needs all the light that is—You!

With much love and light,
Cynthia Carla

I am who I am
Because that is me.
I am who I am
Because that's who I feel to be.

Sometimes
I'm sunny,

Sometimes
I'm cloudy.

Sometimes
I'm grateful,

Sometimes
I'm rowdy.

Some days I'm
casual,
And some days,
dressy.

Some days I'm
organized,
Other days,
messy.

Both thick and thin,
Both sweet and sour—

I am who I am
Every second of every hour.

Sometimes
I'm slow.

Sometimes
I'm fast.

Sometimes
I come first,

And sometimes
last.

Some days I'm
confident

And some days shy.

Some days I'm determined,

But sometimes
I don't want to try.

Both small and great, both boy and girl—
I am who I am, unique like a pearl.

I build castles at the beach.
And splash through rain puddles.
I play all day long
And at night give warm cuddles.

Often I talk.
Often I listen.
Sometimes I dance,
And that makes me glisten.

I am who I am
Because that is me.
I am who I am
Because that's who I trust myself to be.

Sometimes I follow.
Sometimes I lead.

Often I show love,
Which I might also need.

Some days I am open
And some days on guard.
Some days I have fun,
But some are just plain hard.

I follow my heart.
I follow my gut.
I can take the long road
Or follow the shortcut.

Both red and blue,
Both purple and pink—
I am who I am,
A rainbow of ink.

I love my family.
I love my friends too.
I love all of myself
So very much—I do!

I love all the animals,
Insects and trees.
I love life on earth
From the hills to the seas.

I am who I am
Because that is me.
I am who I am
Because that's who I dream to be ...

One day an astronaut,
One day a math teacher;
Maybe an athlete
Or a made-up creature.

I dream of a world
That embraces us all.
I dream many dreams.
Some big ones, some small.

Both light and dark,
Both weak and strong—
I'm a soul who knows
That we all belong.

Sometimes I'm lost,

Sometimes I'm found.

Sometimes I'm flat,

Sometimes I'm round.

I often give hugs
And try to be kind.

I love to share peace
And to speak my mind.

I am who I am.
No box can fit all of me!
Because ...

I am who I am—

and that's who I was born to be!

I am sweet,
I am sour.
I am a body
with magical power.

I am red, I am blue.
I am a spirit
shining through.

I'm a girl, I'm a boy—
I'm a brilliant
soul of joy!

I am strong,
I am weak.
I am a mind
that wants to speak.

I feel sunny, I feel cloudy.
I feel grateful, I feel rowdy.

I like to follow,
I like to lead.
I love to give
But also might need.

I follow my heart,
I follow my gut.
I follow the long road,
I take the shortcut.

I dream of a world
That embraces us all.
I dream all my dreams,
The big ones and small.

I am who I am,
And that's the key.

I'm every type of you.
I'm every type of me.

CPSIA information can be obtained
at www.ICGtesting.com
Printed in the USA
LVHW071331071021
699809LV00002B/29